For a free color catalog describing Gareth Stevens' list of high-quality books, call 1-800-542-2595 (USA) or 1-800-461-9120 (Canada). Gareth Stevens' Fax: (414) 225-0377.

A.G.
For KEN

E.M.
For VEMUND

Library of Congress Cataloging-in-Publication Data available upon request from publisher. Fax: (414) 225-0377 for the attention of the Publishing Records Department.

ISBN 0-8368-1148-8 (lib. bdg.)
ISBN 0-8368-1155-0 (trade)

North American edition first published in 1994 by
Gareth Stevens Publishing
1555 North RiverCenter Drive, Suite 201
Milwaukee, Wisconsin 53212, USA

Original edition published in 1993 by Hazar Publishing, Ltd. 147 Chiswick High Road, Chiswick, London W4 2DT. Text © 1993 by Adrienne Geoghegan. Illustrations © 1993 by Elisabeth Moseng.

Graphic design by Philip Marritt Associates

Editor: Jane Haupert

Printed in Mexico

1 2 3 4 5 6 7 8 9 99 98 97 96 95 94

At this time, Gareth Stevens, Inc., does not use 100 percent recycled paper, although the paper used in our books does contain about 30 percent recycled fiber. This decision was made after a careful study of current recycling procedures revealed their dubious environmental benefits. We will continue to explore recycling options.

Six Perfectly Different Pigs

Written by
Adrienne Geoghegan
Illustrated by
Elisabeth Moseng

Gareth Stevens Publishing
MILWAUKEE

There were once six happy piglets called . . .

Pickles,

Porridge,

Pepper,

Peach,

Presley,

and   Pauly.

Every day they rolled around and played
in the warm summer sunshine.

5

And every night they huddled together asleep in the hay.

7

One day, Porridge noticed that his brother
Pauly was different from other pigs. His
tail was straight.

"Pauly's tail doesn't curl," cried Porridge.

"Whoever heard of a straight-tailed pig?"
squealed Pickles.

"Let's pretend he's not our brother,"
snorted Peach.

So Pauly was left alone. He sat on his tail all day long. Sometimes he forgot and stood up. Then the others would laugh, so he quickly sat down again.

He grew sadder and sadder.

"Oh, please, Mother, make my tail curl like the others'," Pauly begged.

Mother Pig saw how unhappy her little son was, so she tried her best to help him.

That night she rolled a hair curler onto his tail.
But the next morning it was straight again.

She tied a knot in it, but it hurt too much.

She knitted him a curly tail and stuck it
on the straight one. It looked awfully silly,
and it kept falling off.

She curled up his tail with a blue ribbon.
But he still looked different.

"You will always be special to me,"
his mother said.

Pauly was very unhappy.

One day, a purple frog came hopping along . . .

on his way home from the farmyard pond.

"Pigs don't have blue eyes," he said to Pickles, and Pickles closed her eyes.

"Eek! You've got hairy ears," he said to Porridge, and Porridge hid his ears.

"Your snout is too big," he said to Peach,
and Peach covered her nose.

"Where did you get that ridiculous patch?" he asked Pepper,
so she hid her bottom.

"What a peculiar color for a pig," he said to Presley,
and Presley hid in the mud.

Then the purple frog looked at Pauly and said,
"Pigs can't have straight tails."

And the others all snorted,
"Whoever heard of a purple frog?"

But Pauly wagged his straight tail and said,
"We're six perfectly different pigs and one perfectly purple frog!"

And *everybody* laughed.